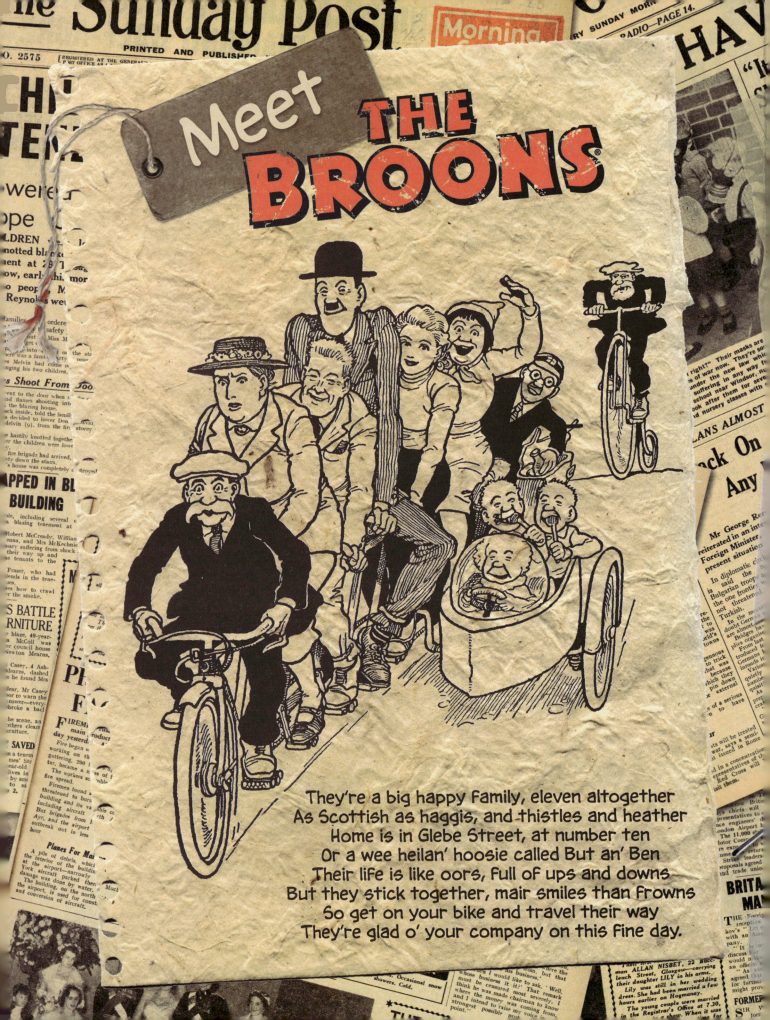

They're a big happy family, eleven altogether
As Scottish as haggis, and thistles and heather
Home is in Glebe Street, at number ten
Or a wee heilan' hoosie called But an' Ben
Their life is like oors, full of ups and downs
But they stick together, mair smiles than frowns
So get on your bike and travel their way
They're glad o' your company on this fine day.

Meet OOR WULLIE®

Let me introduce you tae this fly wee guy
Sitting on his bucket, mischief in his eye
He's no' fashion conscious, aye wears dungarees
Pockets for his treasures and they hide his dirty knees
Poor old PC Murdoch covers Wullie's ground
You've never seen a policeman get such a run around
So often he's in trouble his Ma and Pa despair
But they love every inch o' him frae boots tae spiky hair

Paw Broon's Photos

SOME O' THESE HOLIDAY SNAPS WERE TAKEN WI' MY AULD BOX BROWNIE CAMERA. THEY WERE TAKEN LONG AGO BUT CAN YOU STILL RECOGNISE THE HOLIDAY PLACES? I'VE GIVEN YOU SOME WEE CLUES.

1. THE MOOR IS MORE FAMOUS.

2. THE HOME OF GOLF.

3. THE FURTHEST POINT FROM LANDS END.

4. SIMON AND GARFUNKEL WONDERED IF YOU WANTED TO GO TO THE FAIR HERE.

5. JEWEL IN THE CROWN OF CUMBRAE.

6. HISTORICAL EAST COAST TOWN BETWEEN DUNDEE AND ABERDEEN.

7. THIS ISLE IS FAMOUS FOR ITS CUILLINS.

8. ON THE SHORE OF LOCH BROOM SO IT'S NOT LIVERPOOL.

9. EAST COAST HAVEN SOUTH OF ABERDEEN.

PAW'S RARE WORDSQUARE

Score out the words listed below in the wordsquare as you find them and the remaining letters will spell out a favourite family treat for The Broons. Remember words can read up, down, backwards, Forwards or diagonally.

P	N	R	U	B	E	I	R	O	O	T	S	
A	A	B	M	A	L	E	E	W	N	S	T	
L	M	W	J	A	H	W	A	S	E	K	E	
L	A	O	I	O	E	P	N	S	B	O	E	
O	E	C	R	W	N	L	N	O	N	O	R	
T	O	A	F	A	M	I	L	Y	A	C	T	
M	C	T	R	M	W	I	E	D	T	M	S	
E	L	G	O	T	N	E	H	C	U	A	E	
N	U	M	E	N	H	P	A	D	B	G	B	
T	P	H	O	M	E	W	O	R	K	G	E	
L	T	N	E	M	E	N	E	T	I	I	L	
N	R	I	A	B	E	H	T	N	G	E	G	

ALLOTMENT
AUCHENTOGLE
BUT AN BEN
COOKS
DAPHNE
FAMILY
GLEBE STREET
GRANPAW
HEN
HOMEWORK

HORACE
JOE
MAGGIE
MAW
PAW
STOORIE BURN
TENEMENT
THE BAIRN
THE TWINS
WEE LAMB

GLEBE STREET
9 JAN 55

ANSWER
MAW'S AIN CLOOTIE DUMPLING

Heids You Win!

Wullie's Comic Strips

On a rainy day Wullie and his pals Fat Bob and Soapy Soutar will meet up and swap comics. Sometimes Granpaw Broon will arrive with his really old comics. These are some of their favourite strips.

THREE BEARS

CHEESE! MY FAVOURITE GRUB! I CAN SMELL IT MILES AWAY!

SNIFF! SNIFF!

NO, DAD...

NO NEED TO TELL ME WHERE IT IS — I CAN SNIFF IT OUT....

...IT'S NOT FOR YOU...

SNAP!

AAIEEE!

...IT'S FOR THE MICE! WE'RE OVER-RUN WITH THEM!

HO! HO!

The BADD LADS

DON'T FORGET, KNUCK— AS SOON AS I SMASH THE WINDOW MAKE A QUICK GRAB AND SCRAM!

JEWELLER

THERE — THAT WAS A QUICK GRAB!

SNATCH!

I HOPE IT'S THE MOST VALUABLE THING IN THE WINDOW, KNUCK.

IT FEELS REAL HEAVY, BOSS.

BAH! HE GRABBED OUR BRICK BACK!

DUH!

CLUNK!

HT. 12.4.86

Wullie's Wordsearch

Wullie wants to know if you can find all the words listed below in his giant wordsearch. The words can read up, down, backwards, forwards or diagonally across.

E	T	E	A	C	H	E	R	B	I	F	T	A
B	L	O	P	A	I	R	Y	M	E	E	J	L
S	U	G	R	H	C	O	D	R	U	M	C	P
O	P	C	O	O	R	W	U	L	L	I	E	A
A	A	R	K	O	E	T	R	I	C	K	S	T
P	T	E	I	E	H	A	M	O	O	S	E	U
Y	A	P	E	M	T	S	D	G	R	E	E	L
S	C	C	K	S	R	I	N	B	O	T	R	C
O	K	M	R	O	H	O	O	E	M	D	A	H
U	P	O	S	A	Y	B	S	C	H	B	G	O
T	C	E	R	H	T	U	C	E	T	C	N	D
A	T	R	I	A	H	Y	K	I	P	S	U	M
R	Y	A	F	T	B	A	F	W	O	B	D	A

AUCHENSHOOGLE
BUCKET
CATAPULT
DOG
DUNGAREES

FAT BOB
FITBA
HARRY
JEEMY
MA

MOOSE
OOR WULLIE
PA
PC MURDOCH
PRIMROSE

SOAPY SOUTAR
SPIKY HAIR
TEACHER
TRICKS
WEE ECK

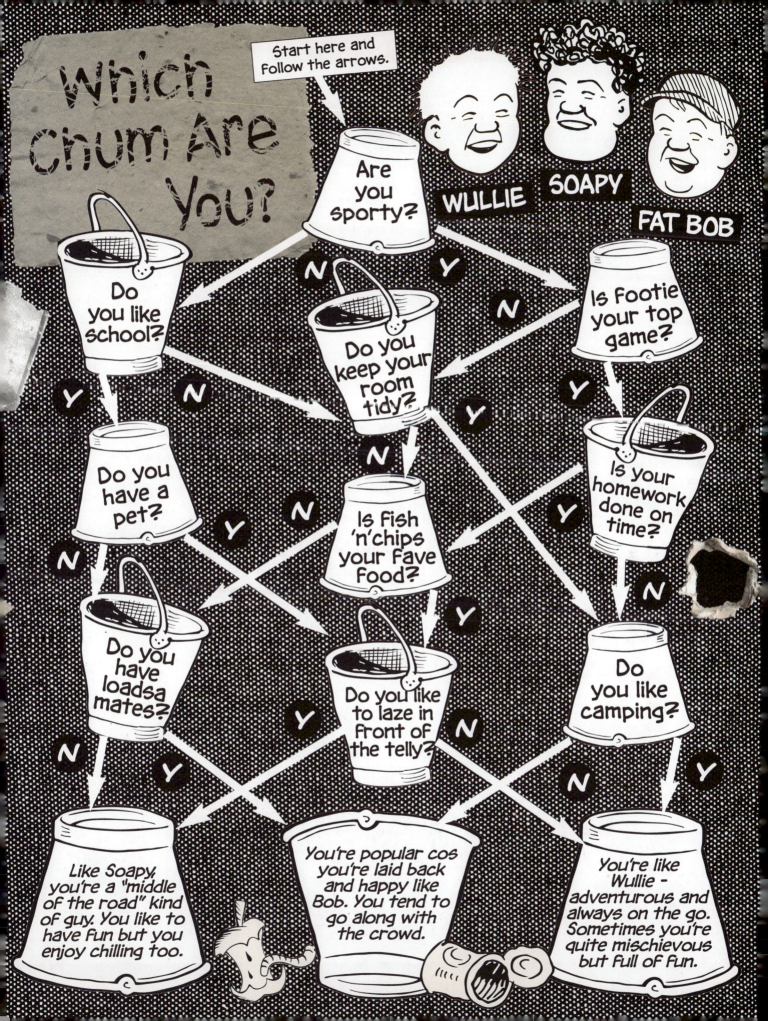

DIG IN TO GRANPAW'S GARDEN PUZZLES

Home Grown Puzzler

FIT GRANPAW'S FRUIT AND VEG INTO THE SQUARES ON THE GRID TO GROW ANOTHER READING DOWN THE SHADED COLUMN. WE'VE GIVEN YOU SOME LETTERS TO HELP.

Word Wheel

HOW MANY WORDS OF 4 OR MORE LETTERS CAN YOU MAKE USING THE LETTERS IN THE WORD WHEEL? EACH WORD MUST CONTAIN THE CENTRAL LETTER AND THE OTHER LETTERS CAN ONLY BE USED ONCE IN EACH WORD. THERE ARE AT LEAST 20. ONE WORD SHOULD HAVE ALL 9 LETTERS

Word Wheel letters: M O N L L A T E T (central L)

Scary Scarecrows

THESE SCARECROWS ALL LOOK ALIKE BUT WHICH 2 ARE IDENTICAL?

1 2 3 4 5 6

YILL   SROPMEIR

Pretty Maids

UNSCRAMBLE THE LETTERS IN EACH SUNFLOWER TO MAKE A GIRL'S NAME THAT'S ALSO A FLOWER.

PYOPP   SIRI

YIDAS   DMLOGRIA

Get Crackin' – THE TWINS ARE HIDING FROM THE BAIRN. CRACK THIS CODE TO TELL HER WHERE THEY ARE.

Code: 1=A 2=S 3=I 4=C 5=H 6=N 7=E 8=T 9=D

Answer:
36 857 2579

THE BROONS QUIZ

QUESTIONS:

1. Name the artist who first drew the Broons page?
2. What is the Broons address?
3. Why were there no Broons or Oor Wullie books between 1943 and 1946?
4. What was produced in their place?
5. How many people are in the Broons Family?
6. What town do the Broons live in today?
7. Which newspaper do the Broons appear in every week?
8. True or False. A copy of the first Broons book sold for over £5000?

9. Who is the family swot?
10. Who is Granpaw's 'wee lamb'?
11. Where do the family spend summer weekends?
12. Which Broon daughter was engaged to be married, Daphne or Maggie?
13. Name the ex-fiance?
14. Who is the eldest son, Hen or Joe?
15. How does the current Broons artist sign his pages?

ANSWERS:

1. Dudley D Watkins. 2. Ten, Glebe Street. 3. Paper was rationed. 4. Jigsaws. 5. Eleven. 6. Auchentogle. 7. The Sunday Post. 8. True. 9. Horace. 10. The Bairn. 11. The But an' Ben. 12. Maggie. 13. Dave. 14. Hen. 15. PD (Peter Davidson).

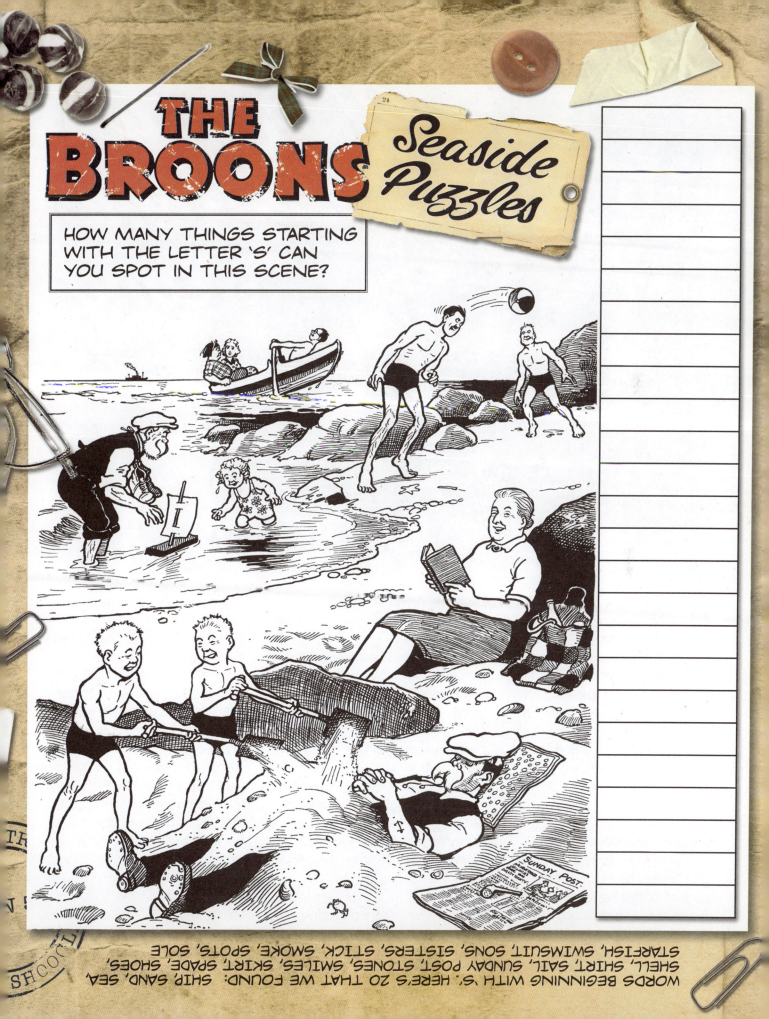

THE BROONS

Seaside Puzzles

HOW MANY THINGS STARTING WITH THE LETTER 'S' CAN YOU SPOT IN THIS SCENE?

Granpaw's Bedtime Story

The Loch Ness Monster

Have you heard o' the Loch Ness Monster, ma wee lamb? Of course you have. A'body's heard o' the monster, and there's mony a tourist'll sit lookin' out ower the loch for hours in the hope o' seein' it and snappin' it wi' their fantoosh cameras. But I'll let you into a wee secret, pet — they dinna ken whit it is they're really seein'.

A'body thinks Nessie's a big monster that lives in the loch, and when she sticks her neck up oot o' the water and gies them that big smile, they think she's smiling just for them. But no! Whit they're seein' is a' a cunning disguise. Oh, aye. The fact o' the matter is, it's really a submarine!

Noo, wha' wid hae a submarine in the middle o' a loch in the Highlands? I'll tell ye, ma wee lamb. It's the Nessies. Because there's no just one monster livin' in the loch, there's hunners! Mind, we . at all, because that maks ye think o' somethin' big and fierce and scary, but the truth is that they're just funny wee folk, even smaller than yersel', and as kind as kind can be.

Noo, I ken ye're wondering how they come to be livin' in the loch. And for that ye'd hae tae ask someone cleverer than yer auld granpaw. Maybe Horace wi' all his book learnin' could tell ye. But ye ken hoo Scotland wis once a' covered wi' glaciers? Well, the Nessies lived in the glaciers, and when the glaciers melted and filled a' the big grooves in the land wi' deep water, the Nessies decided that they'd like to live in the lovely blue water whaur they could play wi' a' the bonnie fish. So they built a little Nessie village in among a' the bonnie plants and rocks doon under the water. And whit a bonnie village it wis, wi' hooses made from stones just like oors. And wee gardens. And then they built a wee school so's a' the Nessie children could learn their letters and their sums, just like Horace and the twins dae. And aye, the Nessie children hae to dae their homework just the same!

And once they'd made their village and their school, and a few wee shops where the Nessie maws could get their groceries, just like your maw goes for the shopping for yer paw's tea, they looked around and thocht, my, but this is a bonnie wee place we've got doon here! It even had a playpark wi' swings and a slide, and a roundabout that whizzed roond to mak the children a' dizzy and the water a' fizzy.

And then one day they were goin' aboot their business and they thocht they heard a noise outside. Now, that gave them a wee fright for a minute, just the way yer maw gets a wee fright when she hears someone at the door until she knows it's Hen or Joe comin' in frae the dancing, or Daphne and Maggie comin' home frae the pictures. Ye see, ma wee lamb, once ye ken wha's makin' the noise ye're no' afraid any more.

So the Nessies decided that all they had to do was see wha' wis makin' the noise and then they'd no' be afraid any more. But how could they do it wi'out gie'in' themsel's awa'? That's when Mayor Nessie — because the village had to hae a mayor to tak charge o' everything, just like yer maw has Paw — Mayor Nessie

thocht aboot it and said, "We need to build a wee submarine so's we can go and hae a look above the water." But a submarine's a kind o' obvious thing to hae stickin' oot the water, so Mrs Mayor had the clever idea o' disguising it.

So once the submarine builders had built it and she could see whit size it was, she knitted and knitted until she'd made it a big jumper to pull ower it. But there was a problem. A' submarines hae a periscope to poke up oot the water so's the folk inside can hae a sneaky peak

WRITTEN BY GRANPAW'S PAL SHIRLEY BLAIR

wi'out being spotted. But they'd built the periscope awfy big, and if it stuck oot the water a'body would see it.

So Mrs Mayor thocht, and soon had the very dab. She rattled doon a few rows o' her knitting' and added on a long neck and a hood to cover the periscope! While she'd been knittin' awa', the Nessie Navy had been learnin' how to drive the submarine, so finally, one grand day, they dressed it in its new jumper and had a big launch ceremony. Mrs Mayor broke a bottle of seaweed cordial on its side, and

then with a big cheer from all of the Nessies, it was on its way. It rose higher and higher in the water, and they watched it get smaller and smaller, until they could hardly see it at a'.

Whit an excitement there was while they waited for it to come back! But whit an excitement there was in the submarine, too, as they got nearer and nearer the top o' the water.

Finally they were nearly there, and at last the captain gave the order: "Up periscope".

Noo, at that very minute there was a tourist sittin' on the banks o' the loch, enjoyin' the view and eatin' his sandwiches, and paddlin' his feet in the cauld water. He was jist thinking that the mountains were bonnier than anything back home in the USA when whit should happen but he saw a wee ripple on the water. He stared, and the ripple got a wee bit bigger, and as he watched he saw a head in a hood come up oot o' the water, and nearly choked on his sandwich!

Bein' an American he had a fantoosh camera wi' him and just afore the submarine dipped below the surface he took a picture. And that's the picture that wis sent a' ower the world. So although we know that it wis just the Nessies haein' a wee jaunt in their new submarine to see wha' wis makin' the noise above them, that's how a'body came to think that Loch Ness has a monster!

Fat Bob's Comic Strips

Bob is never happier than when he has a new comic in his hand, for Bob loves a laugh. The others know which comics are Bob's when they swap for Bob usually has sticky marks from a jeely piece on them.

THREE BEARS

♫ IF YOU GO DOWN TO THE WOODS TODAY. YOU'RE IN FOR A BIG SURPRISE♫ IF YOU GO DOWN TO THE WOODS TODAY, YOU'LL NEVER BELIEVE YOUR EYES♫

♫ IN DRAINPIPE TREWS AND BLUE SUEDE SHOES, BOOTLACE TIES AND RHYTHM 'N' BLUES♫

♫ TODAY'S THE DAY THE TEDDY BOYS HAVE THEIR PICNIC. ♫

The BADD LADS

ALL THE WEEK'S TAKINGS ARE IN THE CIRCUS SAFE, BOSS!

CIRCUS GREAT!

I'VE GOT A GETAWAY CAR OVER HERE, BOSS!

SUPER!

BAH! TRUST YOU TO PICK THE CLOWNS' CAR!

WHAT'S THE RACKET?

BANG!

BANG!

BANG!

BANG!

WHAT'S GOING ON? HEY!

BEANO DANDY

OOR WULLIE's FAME GAME

Oor Wullie's Quiz

Questions

1. Which year did the first Oor Wullie strip appear – 1936 or 1932?
2. True or False. In the early stories, Wullie had a brother.
3. Where do you find Wullie at the finish of each story?
4. Name Wullie's girlfriend.
5. Which of Wullie's friends wears a beret?
6. Who was voted top Scottish icon in 2004?
7. Which constable's beat is Wullie on?
8. What is Wullie's favourite mode of transport?
9. Who owns Wullie's local chip shop?
10. Name Wullie's pet moose.
11. What is Wullie's favourite meal?
12. Where could the public visit Oor Wullie's garden in 1988?
13. Name Wullie's best friend.
14. What is the name of Wullie's home town?
15. Name the burn that flows through it.

Answers

1. 1936 2. True 3. Sitting on his bucket 4. Primrose Paterson 5. Wee Eck 6. Oor Wullie 7. PC Murdoch 8. Carrie 9. Toni 10. Jeemy 11. Mince an' tatties wi' peas 12. The Glasgow Garden Festival 13. Fat Bob 14. Auchenshoogle 15. The Stoorie Burn.

FUNLAND
EVERYBODY'S PLAYMATE

These puzzles first appeared in the Sunday Post Fun Section 75 years ago. Can you do them today?

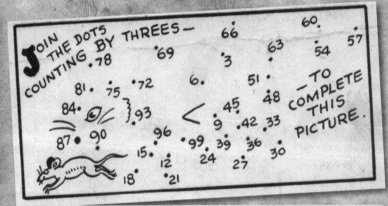

JOIN THE DOTS COUNTING BY THREES — TO COMPLETE THIS PICTURE.

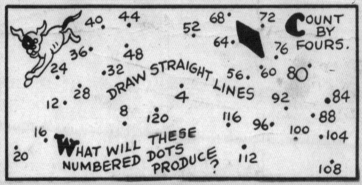

COUNT BY FOURS. DRAW STRAIGHT LINES WHAT WILL THESE NUMBERED DOTS PRODUCE?

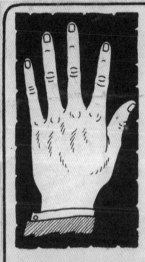

FINGER FUN

ASK SEVERAL OF YOUR FRIENDS TO HOLD UP THEIR HANDS AS PICTURED HERE. THEN SEE WHO CAN BEND THEIR FIVE FINGERS FORWARD, ONE AT A TIME, WITHOUT MOVING ANY OF THE OTHER FOUR FINGERS.

IT SEEMS VERY SIMPLE BUT THEY WILL FIND THAT IT IS REALLY HARD TO DO WITHOUT MOVING THE OTHER FINGERS. THIS STUNT SHOULD PROVIDE A LOT OF FUN FOR EVERYONE.

CHANGE ONE LETTER IN EACH OF THE ABOVE WORDS TO SPELL SEVEN FISH.

1	•	2
3	•	6
7	•	8
18	•	20
22	•	29
31	•	33

60 60 60

Let's see if you can write the 12 given numbers shown above, one into each empty box so that each vertical row of numbers will add to exactly 60.

WHAT CAN YOU MAKE BY ADDING A FEW LINES TO THE NUMBER 6?

See if you can fill in the blanks to tell this Oor Wullie story. We've printed our version at the back of the annual.

MORE Paw Broon's Photos

SOME O' THESE PLACES HAVE FAIR CHANGED OVER THE YEARS BUT CAN YOU STILL RECOGNISE THEM? THE BROONS HAVE HOLIDAYED IN THEM ALL. I'VE GIVEN YOU SOME WEE CLUES.

1. THE GLASGOW FAIR WENT DOON THE WATER TO THIS RESORT

2. 'THE PENCIL' LANDMARK IS SITUATED BESIDE THIS WEST COAST HOLIDAY TOWN

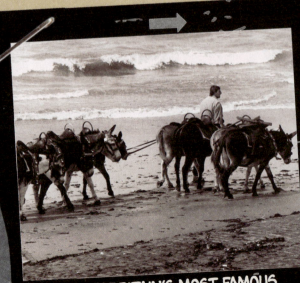

3. PROBABLY BRITAIN'S MOST FAMOUS SEASIDE RESORT

4. SITE OF THIS FAMOUS WHEEL

5. ANCESTRAL HOME OF THE ARBROATH SMOKIE

6. THE CITY OF JUTE, JAM AND JOURNALISM – AND DESPERATE DAN

7. BRITAIN'S HIGHEST MOUNTAIN

8. WEST COAST TOWN THAT IS 'GATEWAY TO THE ISLES'

9. HALF OF THIS CITY LOVES SIR ALEX FERGUSON

ANSWERS
1. Rothesay
2. Largs
3. Blackpool
4. Falkirk
5. Auchmithie
6. Dundee
7. Ben Nevis
8. Oban
9. Manchester

Granpaw's Comic Strips

Granpaw Broon has enjoyed comics since he was a bairn. He remembers the very first Dandy from 1937. He still likes to have a laugh at them yet. Desperate Dan is his favourite.

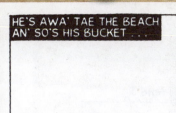

HE'S AWA' TAE THE BEACH AN' SO'S HIS BUCKET . . .

I'M NO' TAKIN' MY BUCKET TAE BUILD SANDCASTLES, THOUGH – IT'S NO' THAT KIND O' BEACH.

I'M GONNA PICK WULKS! MY BUCKET'S HERE TAE CARRY THEM HAME.

THE BEST WULKS ARE AYE UNDER THE SEAWEED.

AN' YE CAN HAE BRAW FUN POPPIN' THE WEE BUBBLES ON THE SEAWEED TAE.

BUT . . .

ACH! YE BRUTE!

SQUIRT!

YE GET SOME FUNNY THINGS IN ROCK POOLS LIKE THIS, YE KEN.

HELP MA BOAB! I'VE SKITED ON THE SEAWEED!

AW, JINGS! THIS IS WEET AN' CAULD . . .

. . . NO' TAE MENTION AWFY NIPPY! OUCH!

BEFORE I START PICKIN' WULKS I'LL HAE MY PIECE – THAT'LL CHEER ME UP.

WHIT A BRAW SPEEDBOAT – I'LL GIE THE MAN A WAVE!

THEN . . .

THE ROTTER . . .

. . . HE WENT AN' WAVED BACK – WI' A BOW WAVE!

WHIT A SCUNNER! I'M A' DROOKIT . . .

. . . I'M GOIN' HAME!

I'VE GONE RICHT AFF WULKS!

The Broons on holiday for the first time.

Both holidays, a sail down the Clyde on a steam ship and a camping trip, were classic working class holidays at that time.

June 28 1936

...e watter " and wish they'd stayed on dry land !

July 12 1936

Oor Wullie's First holidays

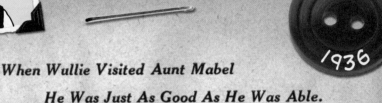

Camping would play a large part in future Oor Wullie stories and was without doubt Wullie's favourite holiday.

Aug 16 1936

When Wullie Visited Aunt Mabel

He Was Just As Good As He Was Able.

Oor Wullie Says—" If It's A' The Same,

When I Have Tae Camp, I'll Camp At Hame."

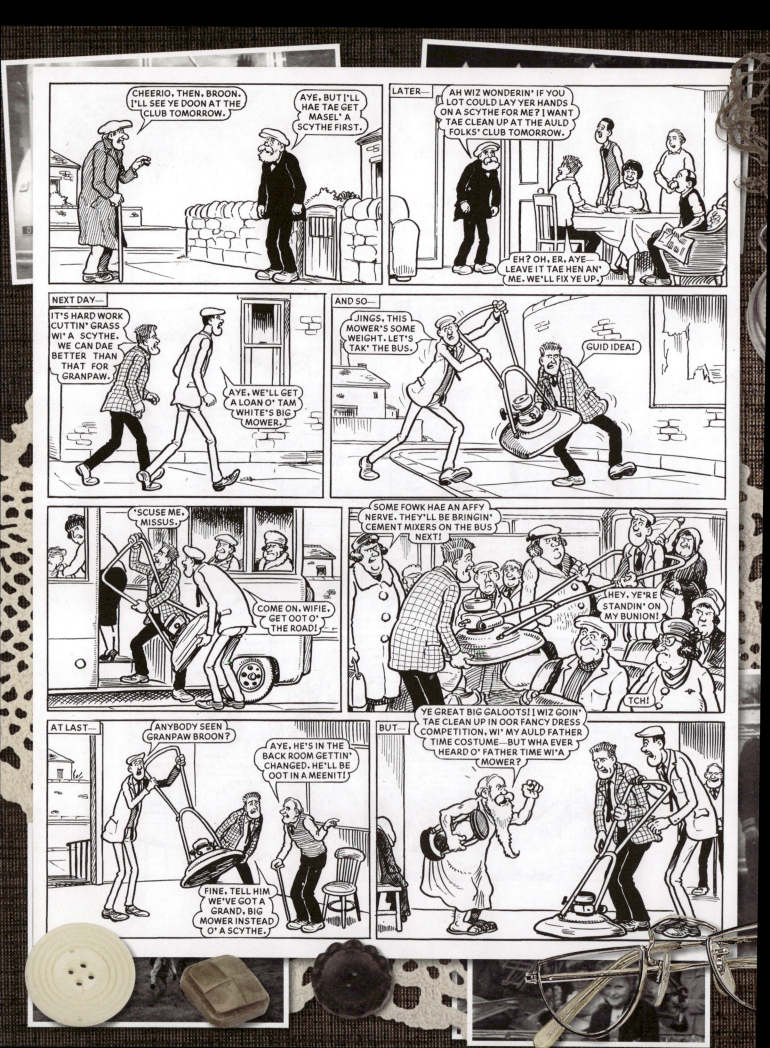

MMM! SOMETHING SMELLS BRAW!

YA BEAUTY — SCONES! MA'LL NEVER MISS ONE . . . OR TWO . . . OR FIVE . . .

BUT THEN . . .

GET AWA' FAE THOSE SCONES! THEY'RE FOR MY W.R.I. COFFEE MORNIN'!

OCH! I MUST STOP WEARIN' MY TACKETY BOOTS IN THE KITCHEN. YE HEAR ME EVERY TIME!

BUT MA'S GIVEN ME A GUID IDEA!

AND . . .

COFFIE MORNING TODAY 10P ENTRY

IF I CAN GET ENOUGH FOWK TAE MY COFFEE MORNIN', I'LL MAK' ENOUGH MONEY TAE BUY MY AIN SCONES!

SOON . . .

YOUR COFFEE, GENTLEMEN. THE FINEST BRAZILIAN ROAST — FAE THE CORNER SHOPPIE!

SOUNDS GUID!

DOES IT? I DINNAE KEN WHIT HE'S ON ABOOT!

BUT . . .

YEUCHS! ARE YE NO' SUPPOSED TAE HEAT UP THE WATER FIRST?

OOPS! BOILIN' THE KETTLE — I KNEW THERE WAS SOMETHIN' I'D FORGOTTEN!

SHORTLY . . .

NO' BAD, BUT ARE YE NO' SERVIN' BISCUITS WI' THE COFFEE AT THIS COFFEE MORNIN'?

BISCUITS? BISCUITS? OH, BISCUITS! ER . . . AYE . . . HANG ON . . .

DOG BISCUITS? ARE YE TRYIN' TAE POISON US?

WHIT DO YOU MEAN? IF THEY'RE GUID ENOUGH FOR HARRY, THEY'RE GUID ENOUGH FOR YOU!

THEN . . .

HERE, WHIT'S THAT UP MY VEST?

HEY! I THOCHT THIS WAS A COFFEE MORNIN', NO' A BEETLE DRIVE!

IT'S MAIR LIKE A CATTLE DRIVE, BOB! THERE'S HUNDREDS O' THEM!

YOU'RE LUCKY WE GOT OOR MONEY BACK, OR WE'D BE CALLIN' THE TRADIN' STANDARDS FOWK!

OCH! THERE GO MY SCONES!

THEN . . .

AM I OWER LATE FOR A CUPPA AT YER COFFEE MORNIN', WULLIE?

I'M NO' HAVIN' A COFFEE MORNIN', P.C. MURDOCH — I'M HAVIN' AN AWFY MORNIN'!

IN THAT CASE, I'LL MAK' YOU A BREW! I'VE BEEN DAEIN' THIS DOON AT THE STATION FOR YEARS!

BRAW!

AND HE GAVE ME MONEY FOR THE TEA! I MICHT GET MY SCONES EFTER A'!

MYSTIC MAW

'MAW BROON'S FORTUNE TELLING SESSION'

WHEN THE LASSIES WANT A BRAW NICHT'S ENTERTAINMENT (FOR FREE, TAE) THEY INVITE THEIR PALS AROOND FOR ANE O' MAW'S FORTUNE TELLING SESSIONS. MAW'S AYE HAD AN EYE FOR READING TEA CUPS.

FIRST MAW MAKS A BIG POT O' TEA AN' THE GOLDEN RULE IS TAE USE *LOOSE* TEA - NANE O' YER TEA BAGS! IT *HAS* TAE BE TEA LEAVES!

THE LASSIES A' HAE A CUP O' TEA AN' DRINK AS MUCH AS THEY CAN WITHOOT SWALLOWIN' THEIR TEA LEAVES. THEN THEY SLOWLY DRAIN THEIR CUPS INTO THEIR SAUCERS, TURNING THE CUP GENTLY FAE LEFT TAE RIGHT (THE WAY YER HEART GOES) AS SOON AS THE LEAVES ARE NEARIN' THE TOP, COS YE DINNA WANT TAE LOSE ANY. WHEN THE CUPS ARE DRAINED, THEY SIT UPSIDE DOON IN THEIR SAUCERS. MAW TAKS THE CUP FAE THE LASSIE ON HER LEFT SIDE AN A'BODY WAITS WI' BAITED BREATH.

HERE'S A SAMPLE O' WHAT HAPPENED THE LAST TIME.

Maggie's pal, Lily, was on Maw's left so she was first to get her cup read...

Maw looked in the cup, turning it this way an' that.

"Mmm," she said. "I see a man waiting for ye, Lily. Have ye got a date?"

"Aye, Mrs Broon. That'll be Stu. I met him at T in the Park!"

"Well, he's no tae be trusted, Lily. Look, he's lyin' squint!"

An' Maw showed Lily a tea leaf that was lying at an angle in the cup.

"Aww," sighed Lily. "He's a braw looker tae."

"Never mind," said Maw. "Now see this big clump o' leaves at the bottom o' yer cup wi' bits stickin' oot like arms an' legs wallopin' aboot?"

"Aye," said Lily, peering into the cup, "whit's that?"

"An' see that shape like an "m" beside it?" continued Maw. "You're gonna meet somebody nice wi' the initial "m" at a big pairty at the end o' the year!"

The lassies were gettin' in a fair fankle.

"Wha could that be?" they squealed. "Matt, Mark, Morris, Max..."

"She hasna met him yet," said Maw, "but mark my words."

When Maw had given Lily mair guid news an' anither warnin' about Stu, the lassie on Lily's left was next. Lily opened her mouth to speak but Maggie quickly stopped her. "It's unlucky to say thank you", she smiled.

Evie, the next lassie, handed Maw her cup. Maw turned the cup this way an' that wi' a puzzled expression on her face. Ye could've heard a pin drop in the room.

Then Maw said, "Are ye goin' on a journey soon, Lass?" Evie's face turned red as she stammered, "N- no…"

Maw looked awfy puzzled as she turned the cup again.

"Ye wouldna' be gettin' married in a day or two, surely?" she asked sounding unconvinced.

Well, what a kerfuffle! Evie burst into tears an' a' the lassies crowded round, trying to comfort her.

"Dinna worry, it's jist a bit o' fun, Evie," said Daphne kindly.

"Whit's wrang?" asked another lass.

Well, it turned oot that Evie wis elopin' tae Gretna Green wi' her lad, Shuggie, in twa nichts' time! Her mum an' dad couldna afford a weddin' so they decided tae run awa' in secret to save them money. Now her secret was out!

"We'll no' tell," promised the lassies.

"That's so romantic," sighed Daphne, dabbin' her eye wi' a tissue.

"But how did ye ken, Mrs Broon?" asked Evie

when she'd calmed doon a bit. "Well, see this shape here," said Maw, pointing inside Evie's cup. "That's you carryin' a suitcase. An' see this circle beside ye? That's a wedding ring!"

"Wow!" gasped Evie.

"An' tae pit yer mind at rest, Lass," added Maw, "a' thae doggy shapes there are faithful friends - probably the anes here the night - so yer secret's safe."

The rest of the readings were less sensational but good fun. Maggie, as usual, had lots of men wanting dates with her. Daphne was coming in to money.

"Aye, it's pay day tomorrow, "she laughed, "an' then it'll be gone."

"Now it's a tea break for Maw while we wash the cups an' saucers," laughed Maggie.

"Whit aboot *your* fortune, Mrs Broon?" asked Lily.

"Aww, it's unlucky tae read yer ain, Lass," replied Maw. "I'll wait until we're at the Fair or Blackpool. "

"But we're no' finished yet," said Daphne. "Maw's gonna read oor cards next."

"An' the cards never lie," said Maw wi' a knowin' smile.

After a wee rest, Maw asked Daphne to cut the cards.

"Now choose nine fae left tae right," she said, fanning the cards out before her. "That means you're getting a kiss," she laughed when two of Daphne's cards stuck together.

Daphne gave the nine cards to Maw. "Mmm", said Maw thoughtfully, "the money that wis in your tea cup…it's no' jist yer pay…you're bein' offered a job."

"Whit?" roared Daphne. "A new job - wi' mair money?"

"That's richt, " replied Maw. "The Clubs here mean there's a man offering you a job soon an' there's plenty money wi' it."

"That canna be right," muttered Maggie. "Daphne's no' brainy."

The other cards gave Daphne some titbits o' news an' a warnin' o' a jealous woman.

"Aye, that's Maggie," laughed Daphne.

Next Daphne had to choose another seven cards and the job offer was even clearer an' comin' sooner. When these cards were read, it was strengthened again with the next five cards which included more details of a shopping spree and a trip over water.

"Maybe I'll be going abroad wi' this job!" delighted Daphne squealed. Daphne wis fair excited when Maw told her to choose three cards and make a wish before handing them back. When Maw got the cards, she studied them and said, "You've chosen high cards, Lass. That means you'll get yer wish."

"What did you wish for, Daphne?" asked Maggie mischievously. "I'm no' that daft," chuckled Daphne. "If I tell you, my wish won't come true".

When it was the other lassies' turn, Evie was assured o' a long an' happy marriage, Lily's man that she was still to meet was going tae be Mr Right an' Maggie had picked nearly a' the Hearts in the pack! She wis gonna be courtin' for a long time!

The lassies had a braw nicht an' jist as they were aboot tae leave, Paw came in wi' a young man. "Oh, I forgot aboot yer lassies' nicht," he said apologetically, "but Billy Buchan here needs a conductress for his bus an' I said Daphne was lookin' for a new job. Whit dae ye think, Lass?"

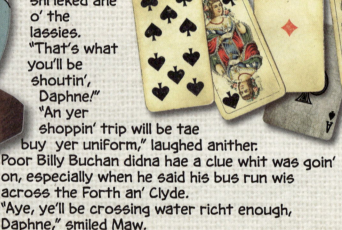

Well the lassies howled wi' laughter tho' some were pretty gobsmacked first! "There's plenty o' money in that job, Daphne!" chuckled Maggie. "Aw, that's no' fair," sighed Daphne. "Fare!" shrieked ane o' the lassies. "That's what you'll be shoutin', Daphne!" "An yer shoppin' trip will be tae buy yer uniform," laughed anither. Poor Billy Buchan didna hae a clue whit was goin' on, especially when he said his bus run wis across the Forth an' Clyde. "Aye, ye'll be crossing water richt enough, Daphne," smiled Maw.

When a' the shenanigans died doon, Daphne told Billy she'd like tae gie the job a try an' he wis fair pleased. "Aye, the cards never lie," said Maw wi' a smile at the end o' a braw nicht's fortune telling session.

Maw's Fortune Telling Tips

READING THE TEA LEAVES

Maw's Golden Rule!
Always use loose tea – nae tea bags!

1. Warm the teapot by rinsin' it oot wi' boilin' water.
2. Put in 3 teaspoons o' tea leaves tae serve 4-5 fowk.
3. Add boilin' water an' leave to fuse for 5 minutes.
4. Pour tea into cups. Add milk and sugar to taste.
5. Drink as much tea as possible withoot swallowin' tea leaves.
6. Drain yer cup into yer saucer, turnin' it gently fae left tae right (like yer heart goes) each time the tea leaves approach the top o' the cup so as no tae lose ony leaves.
7. When drained, set yer cup upside doon in its saucer.
8. The reader taks the first cup on her left and starts tae read the shapes she sees there.

Shapes and their meanings

A sprinkling of tiny, light-coloured leaves is a sign of money. If the leaves are at the top of the cup then you might get money soon. If they're at the bottom of the cup then it could be a long time or the end of the year. Sometimes the tea leaves will form a number which could give you an idea of how many days, weeks or months, depending on how far up the cup the money or an event is.
A dog shape means you have a faithful friend.
A box shape means there's a parcel coming.
Straight tea leaves can be people. Light leaves suggest fair or grey hair while dark leaves mean dark hair. If a "person" is lying at an angle then he/she cannot be trusted.
A lot of leaves together at different angles can mean a party or dance. A circle of leaves alongside suggests a wedding or engagement party.
A big dark mass of leaves is bad news.

NB It's supposedly bad luck to say "thank you" for having your fortune told.

READING THE CARDS

Maw says, "The cards never lie!"

1. The first person should start by cutting the cards.
2. The reader holds the cards, fanned out, and the first person chooses nine cards, taking them from left to right. If two cards slip out together, this means the person will soon get a kiss. When choosing the cards, try not to go back to the left as this indicates that you're regretting something from the past. From the nine cards, the reader can get an idea of romance from certain Hearts, luck and money from Diamonds, work and business from Clubs and sometimes bad news from Spades. They all run into each other to tell individual fortunes.
3. When the nine cards are read, they are put aside and the same person chooses another seven. These cards can tell the same story in more detail or add facts.
4. The same thing happens with the next five cards as they shape your future.

5. Finally, choose three cards and before handing them to the reader, make a wish. If the numbers of your chosen cards are high, your wish will come true.

Some secrets fae Maw

The Ace of Hearts is the trump card of love. Choose this and you'll find your sweetheart.
The ten of hearts tells you that broken hearts mend.
The Queen of Spades warns you of a jealous woman.
The three of Spades says you'll have money and pleasure soon.
The Ace of Diamonds tells you'll marry someone with wealth and brains.
The Jack of Diamonds will draw away any bad luck you've had.
The Ace of Clubs indicates a party within a week.
The six of Clubs says you'll meet a handsome man.

THE BROONS' BRAINBUSTER

SOLVE THE CLUES TO THIS SCOTTISH QUIZ THEN FIND THE ANSWERS IN THE WORD SQUARE ON THE OPPOSITE PAGE.

1. Come here for Smokies (8)
2. A royal residence (8)
3. Regarded by Robert the Bruce as the gateway to the Highlands (8)
4. This place sounds like American money (6)
5. Mountain Range (10)
6. The granite city (8)
7. Scotland's longest river (3)
8. This Rock sounds noisy (4)
9. Famous Falls and house? (5)

10. This town rhymes with "grief" (6)
11. City once known for its 3 Js (6)
12. Famous song by Andy Stewart (1,8,7)
13. A golf town (10)
14. The Bonnie Banks o'.... (4,6)
15. This place is spelt like something you'd eat (5)
16. There's a fair maid here (5)
17. Soldier makes a big leap and a pass here (13)
18. Scotland's highest mountain (3,5)

19. Annual event in our capital (8,6)
20. Where you'll Find McCaig's Folly (4)
21. This county's name is another word for Flute (4)
22. 1314 was the date of a battle here (11)
23. A royal country church (7)
24. Is there a big cat in this glen? (4)
25. Town famous for its honest men (3)
26. Scottish checked cloth (6)
27. A monstrous town? (9)

28. Fife abbey town (11)
29. J.M. Barrie's birthplace (10)
30. Best place to buy a bridie (6)
31. East Neuk Fishing village (10)
32. Prince William met Kate in this university town (2,7)
33. Speed here on a bonnie boat (4)
34. Where will you Find The Riverside Museum? (7)
35. This town's an anagram of "Nigel" (5)

GLEBE STREET
9 JAN 55
AUCHENTOGLE

NOW YOU'VE FOUND THE ANSWERS TO THE QUIZ CLUES, SEARCH FOR THEM IN THE WORDSQUARE BELOW. WORDS CAN READ FORWARDS, BACKWARDS, UP, DOWN OR DIAGONALLY.

Answers

R	E	I	D	L	O	S	H	S	I	T	T	O	C	S	A
I	T	R	A	U	R	B	S	T	I	R	L	I	N	G	W
U	A	S	S	F	N	T	R	C	R	A	T	H	I	E	O
M	R	M	S	A	O	D	W	B	O	E	L	G	I	N	O
E	E	R	E	Y	D	R	E	E	M	S	P	K	Y	A	T
I	H	O	N	R	U	N	F	E	N	T	N	S	C	D	T
R	T	G	R	L	N	I	L	A	T	A	R	T	A	N	A
R	U	N	E	E	F	L	B	B	R	N	U	R	R	O	T
I	R	R	V	M	E	O	A	C	S	D	B	W	N	M	Y
K	T	I	N	B	R	L	E	F	C	R	K	O	O	O	R
C	S	A	I	R	M	I	F	R	O	E	C	G	U	L	A
O	N	C	S	O	L	E	I	A	N	W	O	S	S	H	T
E	A	H	R	L	I	D	T	L	E	S	N	A	T	C	I
B	Y	A	I	R	N	H	E	L	Y	O	N	L	I	O	L
R	L	K	C	A	E	B	X	O	C	T	A	G	E	L	I
N	W	E	S	T	N	E	E	D	R	E	B	A	J	Y	M

THE BROON

ANSWERS TO QUIZ

1. Arbroath, 2. Balmoral, 3. Stirling, 4. Dollar, 5. Cairngorms, 6. Aberdeen, 7. Tay, 8. Bell (Rock), 9. Bruar, 10. Crieff, 11. Dundee, 12. A Scottish Soldier, 13. Carnoustie, 14. Loch Lomond, 15. Scone, 16. Perth, 17. Killiecrankie, 18. Ben Nevis, 19. Military Tattoo, 20. Oban, 21. Fife, 22. Bannockburn, 23. Crathie, 24. (Glen) Lyon, 25. Ayr, 26. Tartan, 27. Inverness, 28. Dunfermline, 29. Kirriemuir, 30. Forfar, 31. Anstruther, 32. St Andrews, 33. Skye, 34. Glasgow, 35. Elgin.

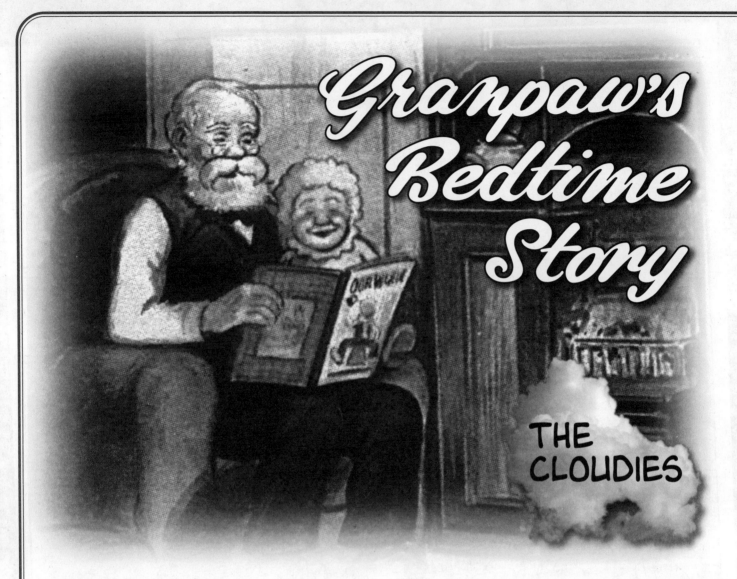

Granpaw's Bedtime Story

THE CLOUDIES

Well, Bairn, so you want your old granpaw to tell ye another story. Let me see now . . .

Your maw says that you've no' been able to play ootside today because it's been raining cats and dogs, and that puts me in mind of a wee tale . . .

D'you ken why we say it's rainin' cats and dogs? There's some clever folk who'd tell you some fantoosh story from history aboot it, but I ken the truth o' the matter. The truth, ma wee lamb, is that every drop o' rain that falls comes down from the clouds, and the clouds are where the cloud fairies live. They call themsel's the Cloudies.

Now, you and me have sat and watched the clouds go by, racing across the sky on a windy day, and we've seen rabbits and cats and dogs and elephants and camels in the shapes o' them, have we no'? But they're no' just shapes, you know, pet. They're the animals that live in Cloudy Land, and when it rains some o' the animals come down inside the raindrops to splish and splash in the puddles the rain maks.

But it's no' just animals that come doon. There are wee children Cloudies too, children just like you, ma wee lamb, and when they see you oot playin' in your wellies and your bonnie raincoat, well, they're just fair envious. So they run around the clouds and find their maws — that's them running a' aboot wi' their wellie-boots on that maks thunder, ye ken. And they ask their maws if they can come oot to play wi' you, and then doon they come, hidin' in the raindrops, tickling the end o' your nose to mak you laugh.

So whit aboot the lightning, I ken you're goin' to ask yer auld Granpaw. Lightnin's their maws showin' them the way doon wi' their torches. Clever, eh?

But it's no' only when it's rainin' that ye' can tell they're aboot. These Fairies are aye up to mischief! D'ye mind thon time we were at the But 'n' Ben and oor Horace had a fit o' the sneezes. He said it was his hay Fever, but it was nothin' o' the sort! That was the Cloudies at their capers again. What they do is shak their pockets to send doon sprinkles o' Fairy dust, and it gets up Horace's nose and afore you know it he's atishooing a' ower the hoose. That maks the wee Fairies laugh, I can tell ye'!

Yer maw's aye happy when the wind blaws Fierce and she can get her washin' oot on the line and dried. But guess what? It's the Cloudies rushin' here and there, playin' their games, and makin' such a wind that it can drive oor Maggie near to distraction, the mess it maks o' her hair.

How d'ye think ye ken when the Fairies are dancin'? Well, I'll tell ye. It's that wind again. Ye ken when it's no' the kind o' wind that just blows straight at ye so's ye're near knocked off your feet but that ither one, the one that tosses the leaves this way and that, so that just when ye think it's blawin' from one end o' the street it whips roond and blaws from the ither. It buffets ye till ye dinna ken whether it's comin' or going? That's when those mischievous wee rascal fairies are hain' a grand dance to themselves, birlin' and heeuching like Hen and Daphne on Hogmanay.

My, but I'd love to be able to see their bonnie faces then!

And then ye ken hoo suddenly it'll go as still as still can be? That's when the wee Cloudies have near danced their legs off and just Fall asleep where they're standin', just like you when you've been runnin' aboot a' day, keepin' an eye on the twins. Ye like to curl up on yer maw's lap and hae a wee snooze, don't you, ma wee lamb, and the Fairies are just exactly the same.

Fog's a right Funny thing that means there's lots and lots o' them a' playin' thegither, a real crowd, like when Joe's at the Fitba and there's just a sea o'

GRANPAW THANKS
SHIRLEY BLAIR FOR WRITING
HIM THIS STORY

faces watchin' the match. Ye cannae pick oot one from another for there's too many o' them.

I ken you like playin' in the snow, buildin' a snowman and stickin' yer paw's auld pipe in its mooth and Horace's specs on its nose, but what do ye think the Fairies are up to when they mak snow? I've heard tell that that's when they come doon to mak magic.

For it must be some kind o' magic that can turn a black road white and mak a'place as quiet as quiet can be, d'ye no' think?

But how do they get back home, d'ye think, if they come doon in the raindrops, because rain doesn't go back up to the clouds, does it? Well, I'll tell you. That's what rainbows are For. When the Cloudies have had enough fun for a spell and decide it's really time they were goin' home for their tea, they get their maws to send down a rainbow and they scramble up it as quick as you like, right up to the clouds, before it disappears.

And then the sun comes out and the skies are blue, and that's when the Cloudies are in their beds, having a sleep until the next time they come doon to play.

So the next time the rain's splashin in yer Face and runnin' doon yer neck, and the wind's tangling yer scarf around yer neck, ye'll ken that it's just those mischievous Cloudies tickling ye and playing chase wi' ye, just like you and a' yer wee pals when ye're playing in the street.

There! Was that no ' a rare story? Now, you'd best be thinking of closing your bonny blue eyes and getting some sleep. I heard on the telly that tomorrow will be a Fine day so you and me will take a walk up Stoorie Brae and see what shapes we can see in the clouds. Maybe we could give the Cloudies a wee wave.

Soapy's Comic Strips

Soapy's mum and dad think that Soapy learned to read by Wullie giving him comics. His room is packed with them and he can remember every story. Swapping for new ones is great fun for Soapy.

FUN in the SUN

WHICH TWO?
These five sandcastles look alike but only two are exactly the same. Which two?

LOST!

The Bairn's lost her parasol. Can you help her through the maze to find it?

WORD LADDER
Can you change ROCK to POOL in 4 steps, making a new word each time?

R O C K

_ _ _ _

_ _ _ _

_ _ _ _

P O O L

YUM!
Unscramble the letters to find The Bairn's fave seaside foods.

CYAND SOLFS
KORC
CEI MAREC
THO GOSD
SHIF DNA SCIPH
DACHWINESS

SHELL SWIRL
Put the answers to the clues into the shell grid to find something The Bairn's making. The last letter of the first answer is the first letter of the next and so on. We've put in some letters to help you start.

1. PUT THIS ON TO PROTECT YOUR SKIN AT THE BEACH. 2. WATER ROUND A CASTLE. 3. PLAY WITH THESE. 4. BIRDS SEEN AT THE BEACH: 5. HEAR THE SEA THROUGH THESE? 6. USE THIS TO BUILD CASTLES AT THE BEACH. 7. RIDE ON ONE. 8. SAILING BOATS. 9. MAKE THIS WITH A BUCKET.

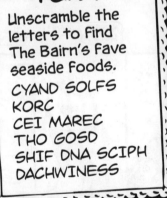

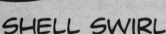

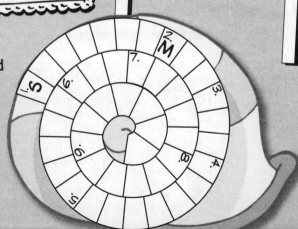

FUNLAND
EVERYBODY'S PLAYMATE

These puzzles first appeared in The Sunday Post Fun Section 75 years ago. Can you do them today?

SHADE IN ALL OF THE LITTLE DOTTED SECTIONS WITH YOUR PENCIL TO MAKE SILHOUETTE PICTURES OF FIDO'S TWO FRIENDS.

A.W. NUGENT

LET'S SEE WHAT BETTY IS FEEDING. SIMPLY CONNECT THE DOTS IN THEIR ORDER.

WOULD YOU LIKE TO SEE THE FEATURED PERFORMER OF THIS ACT? IF SO, CONNECT ALL OF THE DOTS IN NUMERICAL ORDER.

DRAW STRAIGHT LINES TO MAKE A BETTER PICTURE.

Oor Wullie Story –
Here's our version.

WORDSQUARE ANSWERS

Wullie's Wordsearch

PAW'S RARE WORDSQUARE

THE BROONS' BRAINBUSTER

GLEBE STREET

The SUNDAY POST

Here ends the tales frae the Broons and Oor Wullie Some were smart and some were silly

But if it's mair of their fun ye seek They're in The Sunday Post each week.